WHAT AM I FEELING?

Dr. Josh and Christi Straub

Illustrations by Jane Butler

B&H
PUBLISHING GROUP
Nashville, Tennessee

To Landon and Kennedy,
May you feel and love with courage.
Love, Mum and Dad

978-1-5359-3818-1

Published by B&H Publishing Group,
Nashville, Tennessee

Illustration source images from Shutterstock / Jenny Lipets

DEWEY: C152.4 SBHD: EMOTIONS/EMOTIONS IN CHILDREN/CHILDREN

Printed in February 2021 in Heshan, Guangdong, China

3 4 5 6 7 8 • 25 24 23 22 21

Everybody knows that Sam likes to smile. He has the best jokes, likes riding his bike, and loves his dog, Copper.

But one day before school, Dad noticed Sam hunched over his cereal. "How are you feeling, son?"

"I'm fine. I just don't want to go to school," Sam said softly. "I feel flippy in my tummy."

"It sounds like you're feeling **afraid**," said Dad.

"I don't know what I'm feeling," replied Sam.

"Sam, what you feel matters,
but it doesn't have to control you.
Giving each feeling a name helps
you know what to do with it."

"Time for school, Sam!" Mom called. "It's dress-up day! Come get your costume on. And don't forget, today is your turn for show and tell!"

Sam wasn't so sure about show and tell. "Remember," his dad said, "**a feeling is just a feeling. It's not in charge of you**. If you feel afraid, take a deep breath, name your feeling, and ask God to help you with it."

When he walked into Mrs. Stewart's class, Sam felt flippy in his tummy. He felt stuffy in his head. He didn't want to talk. His cheeks felt hot and red.

"Hi, Sam!" said his best friend, Hudson.

"Hi, Hudson. I like your costume," Sam said quietly.

"Isn't it awesome? Astronauts are my favorite!"

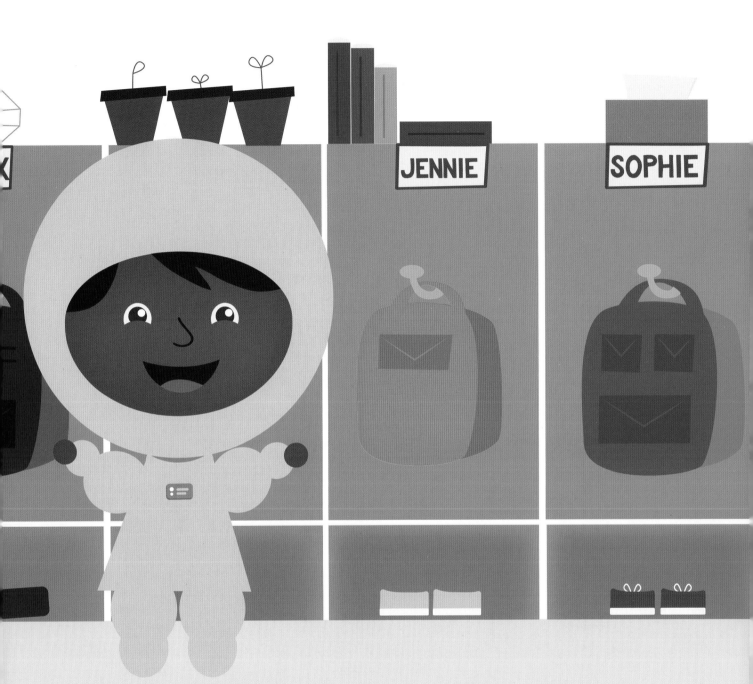

JENNIE

SOPHIE

"I'm so **happy** today," Hudson said excitedly.
Sam noticed that Hudson's feet were almost dancing
and his mouth was one big grin.

Sam then saw Alex in the block corner. "I'm a pirate," Alex bragged, "and I'm building the biggest pirate ship in the world! Ahoy, matey!"

Just then, astronaut Hudson came zooming by,

lost control,

and **CRASH!**

"Oops! Sorry, Alex!" Hudson said quickly as he zoomed off again.

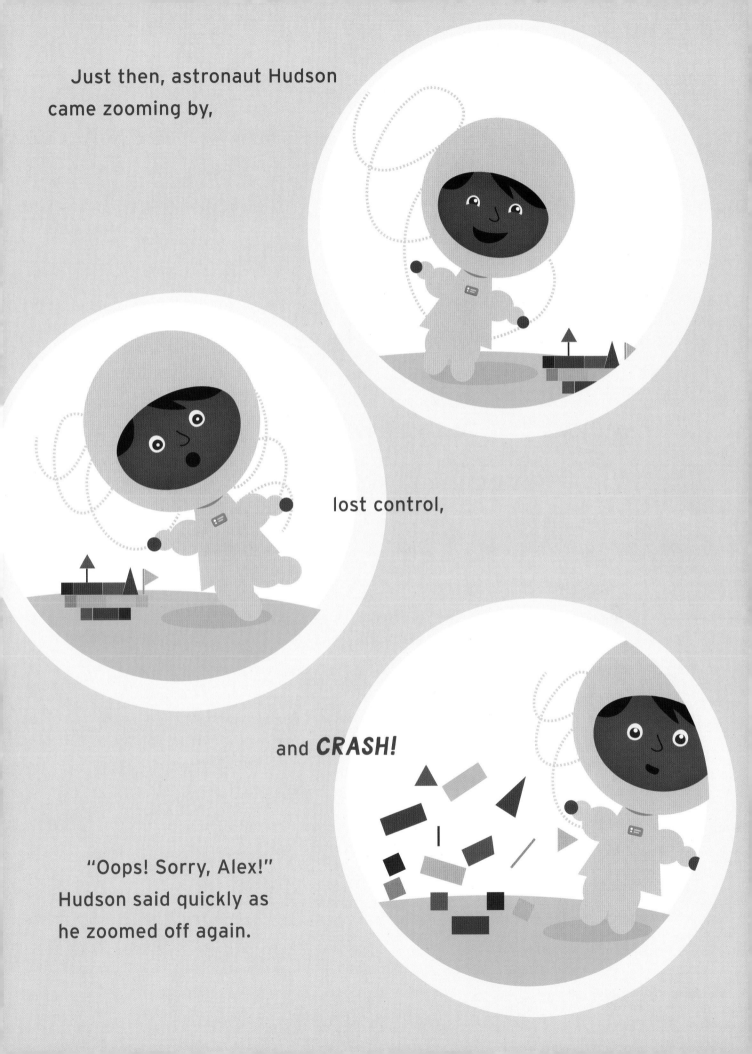

Alex clenched his fists, stomped his foot, gritted his teeth, and yelled, "I'm SO **ANGRY**! My pirate ship is ruined!"

Sophie had seen the pirate ship fall. "I'm sorry about your ship, Alex. Can I help you rebuild it?" she asked kindly.

"No, Sophie! I don't want your help," Alex snapped angrily.

Sam looked at Sophie and saw tears
in her eyes. Her smile became a frown,
and he knew she was **sad**.

Sam remembered what his dad had told him. "Sophie," he said, "it's okay to feel sad. What you feel matters. Take a deep breath, name your feeling, and ask God to help you with it."

"It's time for show and tell!" called
Mrs. Stewart. "Today it's Sam's turn
to show and tell us about one of his
favorite things!"

"That's not fair!" Jennie pouted. "When will it be *my* turn?" She crossed her arms and pouted her lips.

"Jennie," said Mrs. Stewart, "I understand you feel **jealous**, but you can't let your feelings control how you treat others."

"How are you feeling, Sam?"
Mrs. Stewart asked.
"I feel flippy in my tummy.
I don't want to talk in front of
my friends."

"Ahh," said Mrs. Stewart. "You feel **afraid**. When I'm afraid, I take a deep breath and talk to God about what I should do with that feeling.

"Remember, everybody, **a feeling is just a feeling. It's not in charge of you**."

1 2 3 4 5
6 7 8 9 0

"That's what my dad says!" Sam smiled. He whispered a little prayer and bravely stood in front of his friends.

"Today, I'm going to show and tell about my favorite dog in the world! Everyone, meet Copper!"

The whole class squealed as Copper ran into the classroom. Sam told them all about his dog. He even ended with a funny joke that made everyone laugh.

All the friends had learned a lesson that
day about what to do with their feelings.

"Alex, I'm sorry about your pirate ship.
I was so **happy** flying to the moon that
I didn't think about how you felt. Can we
rebuild it together?" Hudson asked.
Alex gave him a high five.

"Sophie, I'm sorry for being mean when I was **angry**. Will you forgive me?" Alex asked.

"Of course!" said Sophie.

"Sam, you were brave to share with us even when you felt **afraid**," Jennie said. "I'm sorry I took my jealousy out on you."

Sam smiled his biggest smile.

Mrs. Stewart told the friends
she was proud of them all.

The rest of the day, they paid more attention to what they were feeling. They gave their feelings a name and thought twice before they acted. They even started to think about what their friends might be feeling too.

After school, Sam couldn't wait to get home.
"Mom! Dad! I had the best day!"

"I figured out why I was feeling **afraid** this morning. I was afraid of talking in front of the class for show and tell."

"But I told God I was **afraid**, and I thanked
Him for my friends. Even though I was still afraid,
I told them all about Copper. When I was done,
I didn't feel flippy in my tummy anymore!"

Mom and Dad bear hugged him.
"We're so proud of you!"
Sam beamed as he threw Copper a
ball. He liked what **brave** felt like.